The Raccoon Who Stole Easter

WRITTEN AND ILLUSTRATED BY

J.P. ANTHONY WILLIAMS

DREAM WEAVER TALES

Thank You - Your <u>Free</u> Gift

Thank you for your interest in "The Raccoon who Stole Easter". You can download your exclusive <u>FREE</u> copy of this amazing <u>Easter Coloring Book</u> by scanning the QR code with your phone camera <u>or</u> go to   https://www.subscribepage.com/easter-coloring-book-fb

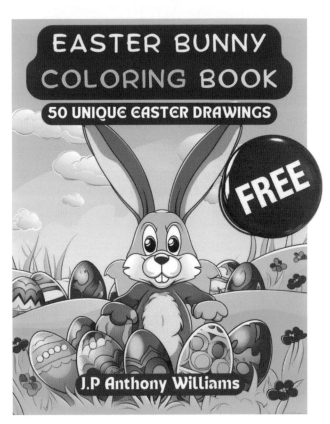

Other Books in the Series
Scan QR Code to check them out

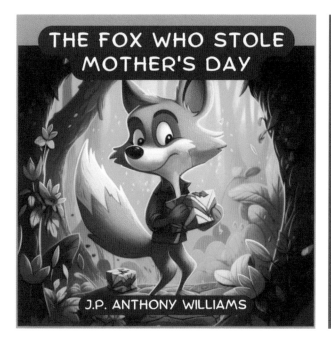

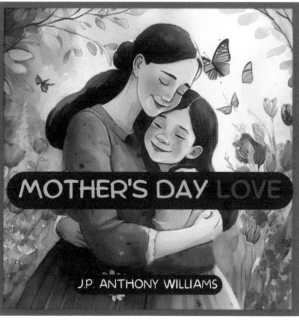

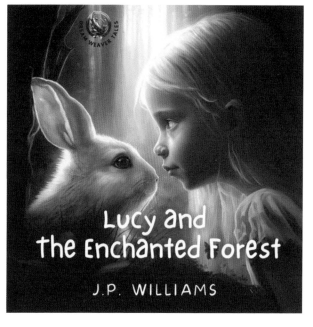

Emma was a little girl who loved Easter, especially going on egg hunts with her friends.

When it was finally bedtime, she curled up in bed with her stuffed bunny and fell asleep.

In her dreams, she found herself in a beautiful forest.
It was filled with vivid colors and soft scents that reminded her of springtime.

As she wandered through the woods, Emma stumbled upon an old path that led up a hill. At the top, she saw what appeared to be a huge Easter egg with a wooden door!

"My Easter eggs are gone! Someone took them during the night," he replied sadly. "I have to deliver them to the children all over the world, but I can't find them."
"Would you like me to help you look for them?" Emma asked

The bunny gratefully nodded, and the two of them began searching the forest.

Suddenly, they heard a rustling in the bushes and out popped a naughty raccoon. The Easter Bunny immediately recognized him as the one who had been playing pranks on all the animals in the forest.

Emma felt suspicious and ran after him. Soon after, she found him sitting alone and looking sad.

Emma, who was kind-hearted, wanted the raccoon to feel better, so she gave him a treat she had brought with her.
The raccoon was overjoyed and grateful for Emma's kindness.

"I've hidden the Easter eggs in three bundles all over the forest," said the raccoon, "You can go look for them; they are not too far away. I know how much you love egg hunts!"
The raccoon then wished Emma good luck and, with a smile, ran off into the bushes before she could answer.

Emma and the Easter Bunny now set out on a wild egg hunt to find the missing Easter eggs.

"Let's start by looking near that big old tree," Emma said, pointing to the large tree in front of them.

The Easter Bunny smiled and nodded. "Good idea! There might be some eggs under those colorful leaves."

Emma then heard chirping coming from a nearby tree. "Birds!" she exclaimed, pointing to an old oak tree. "I think I can spot a nest up there too."

The Easter Bunny nodded.
"Go ahead and check it out," he said.
Without hesitation, Emma started to climb the tree, feeling her way until she reached the highest branch.

As far as she could see, there were Easter eggs! She slowly stretched out her hand and grabbed them one by one, placing them in her basket.

As they continued their journey, Emma saw a small cave hidden behind a rocky ledge. "Look there!" she pointed, her bright eyes beaming with excitement.

She carefully crossed the slippery path to get to the cave's entrance.

"Oh my!" she exclaimed as she rushed inside, where she found another pile of colorful Easter eggs.

Suddenly, they heard a familiar voice behind them. It was the raccoon! "I apologize for being so selfish earlier," he said. "It's alright," Emma said with a smile. "Would you like to join us for an Easter celebration in our garden?"

The raccoon's eyes lit up. He hadn't been to an Easter party in years, and it was just what he needed to cheer up. He eagerly accepted Emma's invitation and ran all the way to the garden.

The garden was beautifully decorated. Easter Bunny pulled out colorful eggs and chocolates from his basket and handed them to the children. Everyone laughed and cheered, including the raccoon, as they played fun games and ate yummy treats.

At this point, Emma woke up from her dream with a big smile on her face. She couldn't wait to tell her family about her dream.

She told her mom, dad, and sister about the Easter Bunny, the raccoon, and the amazing egg hunt. Everyone was amazed by her dream and they all celebrated a wonderful Easter together.

Emma thought about her adventure and understood that being kind can go a long way, especially to people who feel left out.

Above all, she understood that any act of kindness, no matter how small it may seem, will leave a lasting impression on those around us.

THE END

Scan QR code to check out the next book in this series

Thank You - Your <u>Free</u> Gift

Thank you for reading **"The Raccoon who Stole Easter"**.

I hope you enjoyed it and if you have a minute to spare, I would be extremely grateful if you could post <u>a short review on my book's Amazon page</u>

To show my gratitude, I am offering a FREE copy of this amazing <u>Easter Coloring Book.</u> Download your free copy by scanning the QR code or go to https://www.subscribepage.com/easter-coloring-book-fb

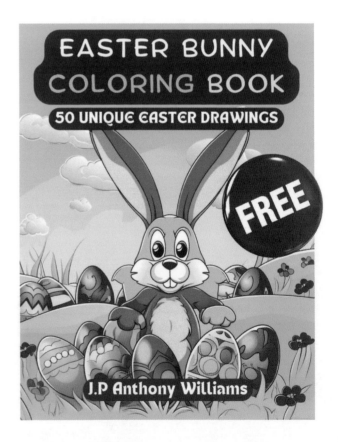

What's Next ?
Scan QR Code for other Books in this Series

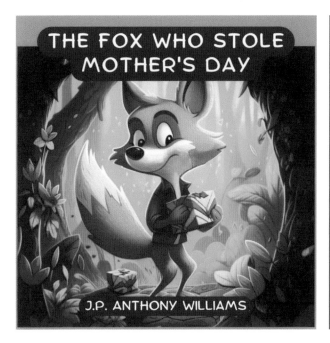

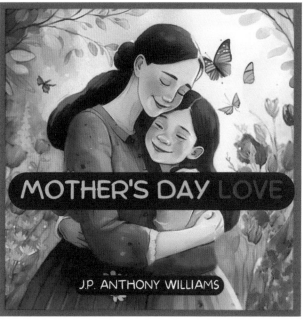

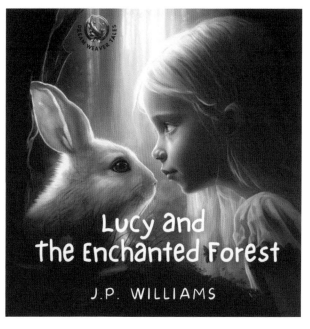

# About the Author

J.P Anthony Williams is a bestselling children's book author, known for his enchanting tales and vivid illustrations. His stories are loved by young readers all over the world.

Born and raised in a small town, J.P developed a love of nature and storytelling at an early age. He spent his childhood exploring the woods and fields near his home, and he loved nothing more than curling up with a good book.

J.P's stories are known for their vivid imagery and richly-detailed illustrations. He takes inspiration from the natural world and from the myths and legends of his childhood, and he weaves them into tales that are both entertaining and educational.

In his free time, J.P can be found exploring new places and seeking inspiration for his next book. He is also a big advocate for environmental conservation, and often uses his platform to raise awareness about nature and its preservation.

Special thanks to my wife and kids for their endless support.

Printed in Great Britain
by Amazon

20837673R00025